MW01264372

ALIEN ABDUCTIONS

by Douglas Hustad

BrightPoint Press

San Diego, CA

BrightP◇int Press

© 2022 BrightPoint Press
an imprint of ReferencePoint Press, Inc.
Printed in the United States

For more information, contact:
BrightPoint Press
PO Box 27779
San Diego, CA 92198
www.BrightPointPress.com

LIBRARY OF CONGRESS CATALOGING-IN-PUBLICATION DATA

Names: Hustad, Douglas, author.
Title: Alien abductions / by Douglas Hustad.
Description: San Diego, CA : BrightPoint Press, [2022] | Series: Mysterious and creepy |
   Includes bibliographical references and index. | Audience: Grades 7-9
Identifiers: LCCN 2021009962 (print) | LCCN 2021009963 (eBook) | ISBN 9781678202040
   (hardcover) | ISBN 9781678202057 (eBook)
Subjects: LCSH: Alien abduction--Juvenile literature.
Classification: LCC BF2050 .H87 2022 (print) | LCC BF2050 (eBook) | DDC 001.942--dc23
LC record available at https://lccn.loc.gov/2021009962
LC eBook record available at https://lccn.loc.gov/2021009963

CONTENTS

AT A GLANCE

- An alien abduction is when a person says she or he was taken from Earth by beings from outer space.

- Two famous abduction reports, one from Brazilian farmer Antônio Villas Boas in 1957 and one from American couple Barney and Betty Hill in 1961, are considered the first abduction reports.

- Aliens and abductions have been common features of pop culture for decades. They have appeared in countless books, movies, TV shows, and video games.

- Psychologists and scientists have studied the alien abduction phenomenon since the 1960s.

- No physical evidence exists that anyone has ever been abducted by aliens.

- Despite a lack of evidence, research shows that people truly believe alien abduction experiences have happened to them. Abductees often go through physical and emotional trauma after the experience.

- Sleep disorders such as sleep paralysis are believed to be one likely cause of abduction experiences.

- People continue to be fascinated by stories of aliens and abductions today.

A CLOSE ENCOUNTER

It is late at night. Crickets chirp through the open window. A breeze ruffles the lace curtains. A young woman lies down to go to sleep.

Just as she is drifting off, something stirs her back awake. She looks around. She is worried. Her glass of water on the nightstand begins to quiver. The whole room is vibrating.

Alien abduction stories usually involve being pulled onto an alien ship.

She throws the covers off to go investigate. But suddenly, a bright white light illuminates the room. The woman can't move. She is pressed back against the bed.

Her eyes dart from side to side to see what is going on.

Through the bright light step three dark figures. They are tall and thin. They have large heads and pointy chins. They surround the woman's bed. They wave their arms, and she levitates.

They guide her floating body to a waiting spaceship. Her body floats up a ramp. It closes, and then the ship zooms into space.

On board, the woman is given a strange medical exam. The creatures poke and prod her. Finally they tell her they don't need

Some people believe aliens have abducted people from Earth.

her any longer. But nobody speaks. She

just hears this in her mind.

And then suddenly she finds herself back in bed. She wakes up with a start. Her eyes fly open. She jumps out of bed.

The audience in the movie theater jumps too. Alien abduction stories like this can be scary. But fans love to see them on the big screen.

SOME PEOPLE BELIEVE

There is no evidence that aliens have visited Earth. There is no evidence they even exist. This means there is no evidence anyone has been abducted by aliens.

But there are people who believe they have been. They believe their experiences

Alien abductions are common in movies.

are very real. They all report similar things

happening to them. Scientists and mental

health experts now study these reports.

They hope to understand the mystery of

alien abductions.

CHAPTER ONE

WHAT ARE ALIEN ABDUCTIONS?

The alien abduction **phenomenon** can vary from person to person. But each experience has the same basic events. They all start when a person is visited by aliens. These are beings who are not from Earth.

Where the aliens come from is not always clear. But it is clear to the abductee that

Aliens are often depicted as short creatures with pear-shaped heads and large black eyes.

they come from outer space. Most often,

the aliens bring the abductee on board

their spacecraft.

BEING TAKEN

John Velez claims to have been abducted

multiple times. He says he has seen several

types of aliens. He calls one type of alien the "grays." They are short creatures between three and four feet (0.9–1.2 m) tall. They have large pear-shaped heads and huge black eyes.

"[The abduction] usually begins with either lights or a humming sound," Velez said.

TYPES OF ALIENS

Many alien abduction reports sound the same. That even extends to the type of beings doing the abducting. Over the years, descriptions have fallen into a few categories. There are the gray aliens, which are short with large heads. There are "tall whites," which are up to ten feet (3.1 m) tall with white skin. A type of aliens known as Nordics are said to resemble people from Scandinavia.

The room will just be flooded with light. Or there'll be this . . . almost electrical feeling to the air. And then I'll either begin to feel very, very heavy—as if I weighed ten thousand pounds, or frozen, immobilized. At that point, usually these little beings—the grays I described—they'll enter the room. And they'll take me on board a craft.[1]

People report being taken in different ways. Velez said he was taken from his bedroom and also while walking home one night. It is common for abductees to describe waking up in bed surrounded by strange figures. People usually report lights and sound during the experience.

IN THE SPACECRAFT

Next, the aliens take the person on board their spacecraft. The person usually doesn't get the chance to explore. Most often, abductees say they are given some kind of medical exam. They recall being placed on a table. Many alien creatures are part of the exam.

Abductees say the exam is hard to understand. It is unclear exactly what the aliens are looking for. They usually don't hurt the person. Often they seem

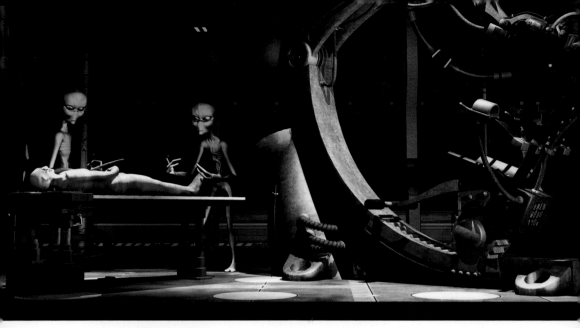

Abductees often describe medical procedures on board alien ships.

interested in the human brain and how the

body works.

Calvin Parker claimed to have been

abducted in 1973. He was nineteen at the

time. He says that he and a friend were

taken while fishing in Mississippi.

"There was what I call an examination

room and the old big ugly creature that

brought me in, he took me and laid me on the examination table and he just backed up out of the way and I couldn't move or anything," Parker recalled.[2] He described an alien device that floated around his head and made clicking sounds.

Abductees say that the aliens usually do not speak. They sometimes don't communicate at all. If they do, they usually do it through their minds. Sometimes they even plant images in an abductee's brain. People describe seeing images of war or natural disasters. They don't understand why they are being shown these images.

It could be a warning from the aliens of tragedies about to happen on Earth.

People report other experiences as well. Some say they were asked to operate some kind of machine. It was an alien machine they had never seen before. The aliens studied how well the person could understand the machine.

KINDS OF ALIEN ENCOUNTERS

The film *Close Encounters of the Third Kind* is about aliens. The title refers to a scale developed by astronomer J. Allen Hynek. A close encounter of the first kind means seeing an alien spacecraft nearby. The second kind involves experiencing a physical effect from the spacecraft. The third kind involves seeing the aliens themselves.

Whatever the experience, the abductee understands the aliens have some goal in mind. They are taking people for a larger purpose. This purpose is not usually explained.

BACK TO EARTH

The aliens then return the abductees to Earth. Usually they find themselves back in the original place from which they were taken. But some may be in a different place. For example, those taken from their cars may be farther down the road from where they were before.

Some alleged abductees report being left in the same spot from where they were taken, while others report coming back in a different place.

Abductees often have a lot of trouble understanding their experiences. They don't know exactly what happened to them. They recall being frightened. They have flashes of memories of what they endured. It is not clear what really happened. But the effects people feel are very real.

Some people even say they have evidence that they were examined. Sometimes people have small indentations in their skin. Others have straight, sharp cuts. Abductees have reported that these things look like surgical marks even to trained doctors.

Some people believe that aliens are able to erase the memories of the people they abduct. For this reason, many abductees can recall their experiences only through hypnosis. Under hypnosis, a person is put

Hypnosis can help people remember things they have forgotten. But it can also create false memories.

into a sleeplike state by a professional.

Some people believe that through hypnosis, they can remember experiences that they normally cannot.

Recalling the experience helps some people. Others are more disturbed by

Alleged abductees can have trouble sleeping after abduction experiences.

the memories. Abductees have reported

depression. Some have trouble sleeping.

They have nightmares about the aliens.

But not every abductee has trouble.

Some people look back positively on their

experiences. Stace Tussel is one abductee

who reported physical marks. She even

says she has had handprints show up on her body. But Tussel does not like the term "alien abduction." She does not believe she was a victim.

"I don't believe I was taken against my will," Tussel said. "I believe that all my life, I've been prepared to share information, to experience information and contact with non-human intelligence."[3]

Another problem these people face is a lack of belief in their experience. They have trouble relating to others. The only evidence of their abduction exists in their minds. But the feelings they experience are real.

CHAPTER TWO

WHAT IS THE HISTORY OF ALIEN ABDUCTIONS?

The term "alien abduction" didn't become common until the 1960s. But people have seen things they cannot explain for centuries. Records of these encounters seem to fit with today's alien abduction stories.

Though they were not always called "alien abductions," strange phenomena have been reported for centuries.

"THREE STRANGE VISITORS," began the headline of the Stockton, California, newspaper from November 25, 1896. The headline continued: "Who Possibly Came From the Planet Mars Seen on a Country Road by Colonel H.G. Shaw and a Companion."[3] Shaw was driving his horse

Some alleged abductees describe aliens as being tall.

and buggy when he saw three strange

figures. They were nearly seven feet (2.1 m)

tall. They had no clothes, just a fine coating

of hair. They carried their own supply of air

to breathe. Shaw reported that the aliens

tried to take him with them. But they were unable to lift him. After that, they returned to their craft and vanished.

In 1957, Brazilian farmer Antônio Villas Boas was working in his field. Suddenly, he allegedly saw an unidentified flying object (UFO) landing nearby. He says a group of small aliens took him aboard the ship. He was sickened by a strange gas and examined by the aliens. They then returned him to Earth. But he had burns on his skin. A local doctor said they were radiation burns. Villas Boas's story is one of the first known alien abduction stories. It received international attention throughout the late 1950s. But it was almost unknown in the United States.

THE HILL CASE

The 1961 abduction story of Barney and Betty Hill was the first case to receive attention in the United States. It established the pattern that many later experiences followed. It began as the couple was driving back to their home in New Hampshire after a vacation in Canada. They suddenly saw a bright light in the sky. The light appeared to follow them. It then circled above them, no more than one hundred feet (30 m)

Betty and Barney Hill claimed they were abducted by aliens in 1961. Their story has become the most famous.

above the car. Barney stopped. He could see it was a spacecraft. There were rows of windows, and gray creatures in uniform were piloting the craft. The Hills suddenly heard a loud beeping sound. They passed out. They woke up two hours later with no memory of the event.

For years they struggled to figure out what happened. Betty suffered from nightmares. The couple researched UFOs. Finally they sought the help of a hypnotist. They believed hypnosis could help them recover their memories. The Hills underwent hypnosis each week for months.

Slowly they began to have memories of being abducted. They remembered that gray aliens took them on board and separated the couple. They were each given a medical exam. The aliens took hair and skin samples.

CELEBRITY EXPERIENCES

Some celebrities believe they have had alien encounters. Actress Fran Drescher believes she was abducted in junior high school. She says she has a scar on her hand to prove it. Singer Elvis Presley believed aliens visited him when he was eight years old. He said they showed him a vision of the future that included Presley performing onstage.

In 1965, a newspaper published the Hills' story. It made headlines around the world. The Hills were not the first people to claim to be abducted by aliens. But they became the most famous.

As their story became more well-known, the mystery began to fade. Betty Hill continued to report seeing UFOs. She spotted hundreds of them. But another UFO enthusiast said Betty Hill was "unable to distinguish between a landed UFO and a streetlight."[4]

Another researcher drove the same route the Hills did in 1961. The Hills would have

The Cannon Mountain Aerial Tramway is located near where the Hills were allegedly taken. They could have mistaken a tramway car for a UFO.

passed numerous towns on their drive. It was unlikely nobody would have noticed the Hills' speeding car. It was even less likely that nearby people would not have noticed an alien spacecraft.

The only evidence was the Hills' memories under hypnosis. Memory was also the only real evidence in other abduction reports that followed. And reports only increased after the Hill case.

STUDYING ALIEN ABDUCTIONS

Research into the growing alien abduction phenomenon began in the 1960s. R. Leo Sprinkle was one of the first researchers in this area. Sprinkle was a **psychologist**. He hypnotized numerous UFO **spotters** and abductees.

Sprinkle became convinced the phenomenon was real. In fact, he came to believe he had been abducted when he was ten. In 1989, Sprinkle left his teaching

R. Leo Sprinkle was one of the first professionals to begin seriously studying alien abductions and abductees.

job at the University of Wyoming. He felt the university did not support his beliefs. He began practicing psychology on his own.

Professionals such as Sprinkle helped make alien abductions a **legitimate** field of study. David M. Jacobs was another.

Jacobs was a well-known historian and college professor. He also began studying abductions. Like Sprinkle, Jacobs interviewed numerous abductees and conducted hypnosis. He founded the International Center for Abduction Research, and the phenomenon became his life's work.

Perhaps the best-known **academic** to study the phenomenon is John E. Mack. Mack was a professor of psychiatry at Harvard University. He had won the Pulitzer Prize for biography in 1977. Like Sprinkle and Jacobs, Mack became

UFO SIGHTINGS BY YEAR

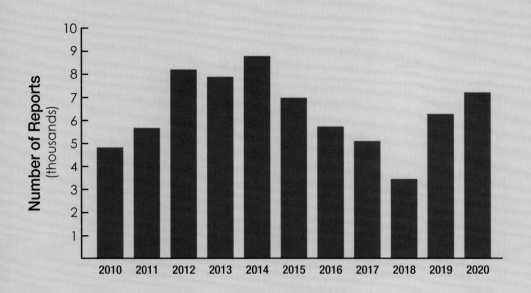

Source: *"Report Index by Month,"* National UFO Reporting Center, *n.d.*
www.nuforc.org.

The National UFO Reporting Center tracks reported UFO sightings by month. Reports fell after 2014 but began to rise again in 2019.

a believer. Unlike those two men, Mack

did not necessarily believe in the physical

existence of aliens. But the experience of

an abduction is very real to the person who

believes it. Mack argued that if it felt real, it was real.

"I would never say, yes, there are aliens taking people," Mack said. "[But] I would say there is a compelling powerful phenomenon here that I can't account for in any other way, that's mysterious. . . . [It] seems to me that it invites a deeper, further inquiry."[5]

Before Mack, people who reported being abducted were usually dismissed. They were called delusional or mentally ill. Mack did not think mental illness was to blame. He interviewed hundreds of people. Many of them had not talked to anyone else about their experiences. Mack wanted to make it safe for people to talk to him. They would not be made fun of.

Mack died in 2004. An institute in his name now continues his work. Its research aims to learn from abductee experiences to understand them better.

AREA 51

Some people who believe in aliens think the US government has proof they exist. They believe the government is trying to cover up aliens. The focus of these theories is a military **base** called Area 51. The base is located near Groom Lake in Nevada. What goes on there is a secret. But there is no proof the government keeps aliens there.

Close Encounters of the Third Kind *was released in 1977. It was directed by Steven Spielberg.*

ABDUCTIONS IN POP CULTURE

Alien abduction is a well-known phenomenon. Aliens have been a fixture of pop culture for many years. The Barney and Betty Hill case was made into a TV movie. *The UFO Incident* was released in 1975. It stars James Earl Jones as Barney. This film helped cement the case in people's minds as a famous abduction story. This is one of the reasons the Hill case was so influential.

The film *Close Encounters of the Third Kind* came out in 1977. It is one of the most famous movies to feature human interaction with aliens. The aliens arrive on Earth in a spaceship as in many abduction stories.

The television series *The X-Files* featured aliens and abductions prominently. One character's sister was abducted by aliens and never returned. *The X-Files* also fueled interest in a government conspiracy to hide evidence of aliens.

Stories of aliens are a familiar part of modern society. For those who don't believe, abductions may seem like a joke. But they are very serious to the people who say they have experienced them. People continue to believe they have

The X-Files *ran for 11 seasons and won five Golden Globe awards.*

been abducted. It is hard to know how

many for sure. Estimates start at several

thousand on the low end. Other reports say

millions of people in the United States alone

believe they have been abducted.

CHAPTER THREE

ARE THERE ALIEN ABDUCTIONS IN REAL LIFE?

The existence of aliens is not impossible. No physical evidence of them has been found. But the universe is a big place. They may not have been discovered yet.

If an alien **civilization** existed, it could be much older than Earth. The beings there could have advanced technology.

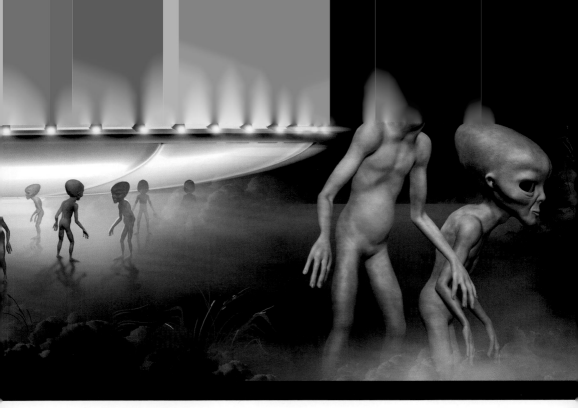

No evidence that aliens exist has been found. But that does not mean their existence is impossible.

It's possible they could be capable of

visiting Earth. But these are all guesses

by scientists. Without evidence, there is

no way of knowing. The only evidence for

alien abductions is a person saying that

it happened.

However, this is not scientific evidence. A person can say anything. That does not mean it's true. Scientists rely on physical evidence that something happened. Despite all of the supposed abductions, there have been no photos. Nobody has managed to bring back any items from on board a ship. There haven't been any witnesses.

SETI

What if aliens exist but don't come to Earth? How will we find them? That's the goal of the Search for Extraterrestrial Intelligence (SETI) Institute. SETI is dedicated to using science to search for signs of life in the universe. It uses antennas to listen for alien signals from space.

"To be taken seriously, you need physical evidence that can be examined at leisure by **skeptical** scientists," said astronomer Carl Sagan. "A scraping of the whole ship, and the discovery that it contains isotopic ratios that aren't present on earth . . . there are many things like that that would instantly give serious credence to an account."[6]

BELIEF AND MEMORY

As Mack found, people believe very strongly in what happened to them. It doesn't matter what really happened. The mind believes that the abduction was real.

Mack found that mental illness was not to blame for these beliefs. But an abduction experience can have real physical and mental health effects. People often experience post-traumatic stress disorder (PTSD) when reliving the experience. People are very serious in talking about their experiences. They get emotional. Some even have physical effects. They may experience nausea, faintness, and blurry vision.

"My criterion for including or crediting an observation by an abductee," Mack wrote, "is simply whether what has been reported

50

Even if a person was not actually abducted by aliens, the mental health effects of the experience can be very real.

was felt to be real by the experiencer

and was communicated sincerely and

authentically to me."[7]

Researchers think that belief in abduction

is a form of false memory. This is the belief

that something that feels real in a person's

Sleep disorders could explain why many abduction stories involve the abductee being taken from bed.

mind actually happened when it did not.

Hypnosis may create false memories.

WHAT CAUSES ABDUCTION EXPERIENCES?

The cause of abduction experiences is

still a mystery. One common theory is

sleep paralysis. Sleep paralysis is a sleep disorder. It affects as much as 40 percent of the population. In sleep paralysis, a person is asleep. Her eyes are open. She is aware of her surroundings. But she is unable to move. Some sufferers also **hallucinate**. These visions are often frightening. These things together could explain a belief in alien abduction.

Another possible explanation is lucid dreaming. Half of all people will have a lucid dream at some point in their lives. A lucid dream is like a regular dream. But the dreamer has control over the dream.

People who are familiar with aliens may imagine seeing them when experiencing sleep paralysis.

He can move around within the dream and do as he wishes.

Most people report being abducted from bed. It makes sense that a sleep disorder may be to blame. But sleep disorders are fairly common. Not all people with sleep disorders believe they were abducted by aliens. There are further factors that may make a person more likely to believe he or she was abducted. One is how likely a person is to believe strange events have a paranormal explanation. Another is a person's culture. People experiencing sleep paralysis often report seeing an evil force. The evil force a person describes often changes based on culture. It makes sense that someone familiar with aliens would envision an evil creature as an alien.

THE POWER OF SUGGESTION

One thing often cited as evidence that abductions are real is that people often tell similar stories. The basic outline of each abduction is the same. But researchers believe this is due to hearing other stories first. Or it could be due to seeing abductions in movies and TV shows. Alien abduction stories are easy to find today. But that wasn't true when the stories first began to appear. Still, even the most famous stories may have their sources in pop culture.

Space exploration began in the 1950s. Many people were interested in space. In 1957, a Brazilian writer wrote a flying saucer story for a magazine. Antônio Villas Boas

Many abduction stories have elements in common, such as being in a car when taken. People could be influenced by other stories when they describe abduction experiences.

claimed to have been abducted one day

after he read this story. And a sketch he

made of the spacecraft looked a lot like the

Russian satellite *Sputnik*. *Sputnik* launched

in 1957.

Betty Hill's sister had previously reported

seeing a UFO. That gave Betty the idea

that the light following her and Barney

was an alien spacecraft. She may have

mistaken nightmares for memories of

being abducted.

Research shows that a person's past

may influence what he or she experiences.

Barney Hill was a veteran of World War II

LIFE ON MARS?

The planet Mars has long been identified as a planet that could have life on it. It is similar to Earth in many ways. So far, no true evidence has surfaced to indicate life. But there are signs that scientists simply haven't found it yet. In September 2020, NASA discovered three large underground lakes. The presence of liquid water could mean something lives on Mars.

(1939–1945). The German dictator during the war, Adolf Hitler, was a well-known figure. Hill later recalled that the alien leader looked like Hitler.

Betty Hill was more positive about meeting the aliens. She recalled joking with them. She said one even gave her a book to take back with her. But the others wouldn't allow it.

There are several things most alleged abductees have in common. Usually they already believe in aliens and UFOs. They often are American. Most reports tend to come from the United States.

The International UFO Museum and Research Center in Roswell, New Mexico, features dioramas and other information about UFOs.

Researchers also report that abductees have active imaginations. These are all trends. But no one factor predicts abduction belief for sure.

Researchers believe that most people truly believe their abduction stories. They do not make up stories for attention or money. But there are exceptions. One notable hoax came from Travis Walton in 1975. Walton received a large cash prize by selling his story to a newspaper. But discrepancies in his story led experts to believe it was invented.

Aliens may not be actually abducting people. But that doesn't mean that people who say they were abducted are lying. What has actually happened to these people remains a mystery.

CHAPTER FOUR

WHAT ALIEN ABDUCTION STORIES ARE TOLD TODAY?

Alien abduction stories have been around since the 1950s. UFO sightings go back even farther. They have been a part of life for a long time. But there is evidence that these stories are becoming rarer. Websites that track UFO sightings

Alien abduction stories in the media are rarer than they once were.

showed a decline beginning in 2014. By

2018, reports were half of what they were in

2014. But UFO sightings began increasing

again in 2019 and 2020.

Statistics on reported abductions are harder to find than those on UFOs. But abduction stories used to make news. Now they are mostly just told among UFO enthusiasts.

Evidence shows the public may simply be tired of aliens. In the 1980s and 1990s, scholars wrote books on alien abductions. These books were the first scholarly research on the subject. It was new information to the public. People now have access to even more information. They can read about medical causes for abduction beliefs. There is less mystery.

It is hard for something to remain a
mystery today. Smartphones are common.
It is easier than ever to take photos or video.
People expect to see evidence. It is too
hard to believe a supernatural event could
go unnoticed.

SPACE PHENOMENA ON CAMERA

Video cameras are nearly everywhere in
today's world. They are always ready to record
mysterious sights from space. In 2013, a
meteorite fell to Earth in Russia. It exploded,
damaging buildings and injuring people. Many
people in Russia use video cameras on the
dashboards of their cars. Many cameras caught
the asteroid strike. It was the first time this kind
of event was widely captured on film.

Many alleged abductees share their experiences in online communities.

But there still are people who believe. There are many websites and groups for people interested in alien abductions. Most discussion happens away from the public.

"I think there are just as many people who believe that these things happen, but I think that they've retreated from public view and they just talk to themselves," said UFO researcher David Clarke. "In order for you to be a party to that, you need to buy into that reality."[8]

ABDUCTIONS IN MODERN MEDIA

Alien abductions are still popular in movies and TV. But the stories have changed over time. They are often more fantastical or lighthearted. The 2014 film *Guardians of the Galaxy* is one example. Peter Quill gets abducted by space pirates as a child. He becomes the leader of a band of outlaws. They are called the Guardians of the Galaxy. He calls himself Star-Lord. The film shows an entire universe of alien creatures.

Alien abductions are even depicted for younger audiences. The 2011 film *Mars Needs Moms* is about Martians who abduct a boy and his mother. They need the mother's parenting skills to help raise young Martians.

Star-Lord is played by Chris Pratt in the Guardians of the Galaxy movies.

These lighthearted stories show that alien

abductions are not taken very seriously in

modern society. They are often treated as

a joke. A series of sketches on the comedy

show *Saturday Night Live* is one example.

Actor Ryan Gosling's character claimed to

ROSWELL

One incident in 1947 kicked off public interest in
UFOs. People claimed a flying saucer crashed
near Roswell, New Mexico. They believed the
government covered up the evidence. The
"flying saucer" was actually a weather balloon.
It came from the nearby Air Force base.
But some people still believe. Roswell has
embraced aliens as part of its culture.

be abducted by aliens. *SNL* cast members Cecily Strong and Kate McKinnon also played abductees.

But people do still believe in aliens. In a 2015 poll, more than half of people surveyed in the United States said they believed in aliens. It is possible abduction stories will continue to be told. They just may be different.

"The ideas about UFOs and aliens continue to evolve as we project our social and cultural ideas on them," said paranormal researcher Sharon Hill. "Since we have no single easy explanation for

Alien abduction stories will continue to evolve as people's ideas about aliens change.

all these claims regarding the decline in

sightings, the future vision of [UFO studies]

seems rather open-ended. I don't think it's

dead, just changing."[9]

GLOSSARY

academic

a person whose background is in education

base

a military unit's home location, where people train, work, and sometimes live

civilization

a complete society with things like culture, science, and government

hallucinate

to see things that are not really there

legitimate

real or authentic

phenomenon

an event that can be observed

psychologist

a person who studies the human mind

skeptical

unsure of something's authenticity

spotters

people who watch for certain things, such as UFOs

SOURCE NOTES

CHAPTER ONE: WHAT ARE ALIEN ABDUCTIONS?

1. Quoted in "Interview with John Velez," *PBS NOVA: Kidnapped by UFOs?* n.d. www.pbs.org.

2. Quoted in Shelby Myers and David Rencher, "The Alien Abduction," *Fox10 News*, January 14, 2019. www.fox10tv.com.

CHAPTER TWO: WHAT IS THE HISTORY OF ALIEN ABDUCTIONS?

3. Quoted in Michael Fitzgerald, "Fitzgerald: The Day Space Aliens Visited Stockton," *Recordnet.com*, March 26, 2015. www.recordnet.com.

4. Quoted in Brian Dunning, "Betty and Barney Hill: The Original UFO Abduction," *Skeptoid Podcast*, October 21, 2008. http://skeptoid.com.

5. Quoted in Angela Hind, "Alien Thinking," *BBC News*, June 8, 2005. http://news.bbc.co.uk.

CHAPTER THREE: ARE THERE ALIEN ABDUCTIONS IN REAL LIFE?

6. Quoted in "Interview with Carl Sagan: Author, Astronomer," *PBS NOVA: Kidnapped by UFOs?* n.d. www.pbs.org.

7. Quoted in Niall Boyce, "The Psychiatrist Who Wanted to Believe," *The Lancet*, 380, no. 9848 (2012): 1140–1141. www.thelancet.com.

CHAPTER FOUR: WHAT ALIEN ABDUCTION STORIES ARE TOLD TODAY?

8. Quoted in Lisa Rodriguez McRobbie, "Why Alien Abductions Are Down," *Boston Globe*, June 12, 2016. www.bostonglobe.com.

9. Quoted in Philip Jaekl, "What Is Behind the Decline in UFO Sightings?" *Guardian*, September 21, 2018. www.theguardian.com.

FOR FURTHER RESEARCH

BOOKS

Megan Borgert-Spaniol, *UFOs: Are Alien Aircraft Overhead?* Minneapolis, MN: Abdo Publishing, 2019.

Virginia Loh-Hagan, *Extraterrestrial Life*. Ann Arbor, MI: Cherry Lake Publishing, 2021.

Arnold Ringstad, *UFOs and Aliens*. Mankato, MN: The Child's World, 2021.

INTERNET SOURCES

"Do You Believe in UFOs?" *Wonderopolis*, n.d. www.wonderopolis.org.

Samuel Levin, "Curious Kids: What Would Aliens Be Like?" *The Conversation*, November 20, 2019. http://theconversation.com.

"What Exactly Are UFOs?" *CBC Kids,* n.d. www.cbc.ca.

WEBSITES

Finding Our Place in the Cosmos: From Galileo to Sagan and Beyond
www.loc.gov/collections/finding-our-place-in-the-cosmos-with-carl-sagan/about-this-collection/

The "Finding Our Place in the Cosmos" collection from the Library of Congress explores how humans have thought of the universe throughout time, including ideas about alien life. The collection contains manuscripts, articles, movie posters, and more.

NASA Science: Solar System Exploration
http://solarsystem.nasa.gov

The study of space and the universe could one day uncover alien life. NASA's Solar System Exploration encyclopedia allows users to learn more about the solar system and deep space exploration.

SETI Institute
www.seti.org

The website of the Search for Extraterrestrial Intelligence (SETI) Institute allows users to learn about real-life searches for aliens.

INDEX

IMAGE CREDITS

ABOUT THE AUTHOR

Douglas Hustad is a freelance author who focuses primarily on science and history books for young people. He, his wife, and their two dogs live in the northern suburbs of San Diego, California.